This book belongs to:

....

....

Quarto is the authority on a wide range of topics.

Quarto educates, entertains and enriches the lives of our readers—enthusiasts and lovers of hands-on living.

www.quartoknows.com

Author: Amanda Askew
Illustrator: Davide Ortu
Designer: Victoria Kimonidou
Editor: Ellie Brough

© 2018 Quarto Publishing plc

First Published in 2018 by QED Publishing,
an imprint of The Quarto Group.
The Old Brewery, 6 Blundell Street,
London N7 9BH, United Kingdom.
T (0)20 7700 6700 F (0)20 7700 8066
www.QuartoKnows.com

A catalogue record for this book is available from
the British Library.

ISBN 978 1 78493 213 8

Manufactured in Dongguan, China TL112017

9 8 7 6 5 4 3 2 1

MIX
Paper from
responsible sources
FSC® C104723

Cinderella

Written by Amanda Askew
Illustrated by Davide Ortu

There once lived a girl who was kind and sweet.
She lived with her stepmother and two
stepsisters. All three were mean and unkind.

They treated the girl
cruelly. Her day was
filled with hard work...

...her dinner was scraps
and her clothes were rags.

At night, she slept
by the dying fire for
warmth and would wake
up covered in cinders.

She soon became known as Cinderella.

One day an invitation came from the palace.
The prince was to hold a ball for all of the young
ladies in the land so that he could choose a wife.

His Royal
Highness,
the Prince, invites
you to a ball.

"Can I go to the ball too?"
Cinderella asked her stepsisters.

The eldest smiled
meanly and spilled a bag
of lentils in the fireplace.

"If you can pick out all of
the lentils in an hour,
you may go to the ball."

Cinderella sang as she worked.
She sang so sweetly that the birds
and mice heard and came in to help.

And within the hour, all of the lentils had been collected.

The stepsisters returned dressed for the ball.

"I did it!" Cinderella cried happily. "Now I can go to the ball!"

But the stepsisters laughed cruelly, "You?
Go to the ball? Don't be silly, you would embarrass us."
And without another word they left.

Cinderella ran outside and sobbed.

She had all but given up hope of ever being happy when, suddenly, with a flash and a POP a fairy appeared before her.

"Don't be alarmed, Cinderella," said the fairy. "I am your Fairy Godmother and I'm here to tell you, you shall go to the ball!"

Cinderella was stunned. "But how?" she asked.

"Simple!" replied her Fairy Godmother. "Fetch me a pumpkin, six mice, six lizards and a goose."

Cinderella did as she was told.
Her Fairy Godmother pulled out a wand
and with a **flick** and a **swish...**

...the pumpkin became a glittering, golden carriage;
the mice: six speckled grey horses...

...the lizards: her courteous footmen,
and the goose: her handsome driver.

"Now it's your turn," her Fairy Godmother said. And with another flourish of her wand, Cinderella's rags became a beautiful dress that shone like diamonds.

Pretty glass slippers appeared on her dainty feet.

"There is one condition," said the Fairy Godmother.
"The magic will end at the last stroke of midnight.
You must be home by then."

"I will. Thank you, Fairy Godmother,"
beamed Cinderella.

When Cinderella arrived at the ball, everyone turned to stare at her, including her stepsisters. They did not recognise her in all the finery.

Everyone thought she was a beautiful princess from a faraway land.

The prince fell in love
with her instantly and
danced with her all night.

All too soon the clock
struck midnight.

"Oh," Cinderella
exclaimed. "I must go!"

As she ran down the stairs,
one of her slippers fell off.

The prince chased after her but she was gone.
He picked up the glass slipper and vowed:
"I will find the girl whose foot fits this
slipper. I will find her and I will marry her."

The prince tried the slipper on every girl
in the land, but it didn't fit anybody.

Finally, he came to Cinderella's house. Both the stepsisters
tried the slipper but their feet were too big.

"May I try?"
Cinderella asked.

"You?" her sisters laughed.
"You weren't at the ball."

The prince looked at the shy servant
girl and offered her the slipper.

It fitted perfectly.
"You are my love!"
the prince exclaimed.

The prince and Cinderella were
married soon after.

Cinderella forgave her stepsisters for their unkindness and she ruled as a kind and fair Queen.

Next Steps

Discussion and comprehension

Ask the children the following questions and discuss their answers:

• Why was the girl in the story called Cinderella?

• What things did the Fairy Godmother ask Cinderella to fetch?

• What did Cinderella wear on her feet to the ball? What time did she have to be home?

• Did this story have a happy ending for everybody?

Freeze-frame

Enlarge a copy of the page showing the stepsister trying on the glass slipper. Cover the text so it is a freeze-framed scene. Ask the children to tell you what the stepsister is doing in the picture and what she might be feeling. For example, the stepsister is sitting in the chair and feeling cross because the slipper doesn't fit her foot. Ask the children to write a sentence saying what one of the other characters is doing. Then if they are able, ask them to write a second sentence about how that character might be feeling. Ask them to share their sentences.

Make a golden carriage

Give each child a large, gold-coloured paper plate. Cut out two circles of black card and stick them to the bottom of the plate for the wheels. Cut out two further shapes to stick on the top half of the plate for the windows. Give the children a small, colour photocopied picture of Cinderella to stick on one of the windows. Finally, give them lots of shiny stars and stickers to finish their decoration.